Para Teresa — JL

Por tener cuatro años, y para
mi adorable musa — MS

For Teresa — JL

To being four years old, and to
my adorable muse — MS

Text copyright © 2014 by Jorge Luján
Illustrations copyright © 2013 by Mandana Sadat
English translation copyright © 2014 by Elisa Amado
First published in a bilingual English and Spanish edition in
Canada and the USA in 2014 by Groundwood Books

Groundwood Books / House of Anansi Press
110 Spadina Avenue, Suite 801, Toronto, Ontario M5V 2K4
or c/o Publishers Group West
1700 Fourth Street, Berkeley, CA 94710

We acknowledge for their financial support of our publishing
program the Government of Canada through the Canada
Book Fund (CBF).

Library and Archives Canada Cataloguing in Publication
Luján, Jorge, author
Moví la mano = I moved my hand / written by Jorge
Luján ; illustrated by Mandana Sadat ; translated by Elisa
Amado.
Text in Spanish and English.
Issued in print and electronic formats.
ISBN 978-1-55498-485-5 (bound).—
ISBN 978-1-55498-740-5 (pdf)
I. Amado, Elisa, translator II. Sadat, Mandana, illustrator
III. Title. IV. Title: I moved my hand.
PZ73.L85Mo 2014   j861'.7   C2014-901372-8

The illustrations were done in a combination of color pencil,
ink, crayon and digital techniques.
Design by Michael Solomon
Printed and bound in Malaysia

FSC
www.fsc.org
MIX
Paper from
responsible sources
FSC® C012700

Jorge Luján

Mandana Sadat

Moví la mano
I Moved My Hand

Traducción de / Translated by
Elisa Amado

Groundwood Books
House of Anansi Press
Toronto   Berkeley

Moví la mano y
encontré un coco.

I moved my hand and
I found a coconut.

Agité el coco
y encontré un lago.

I shook the coconut
and I found a lake.

Revolví el lago y
encontré un pez.

I stirred the lake
and I found a fish.

Hice girar al pez
y encontré la luna.

I swirled the fish and
I found the moon.

Toqué la luna y rodó en el cielo.

I touched the moon
and it rolled through the night.

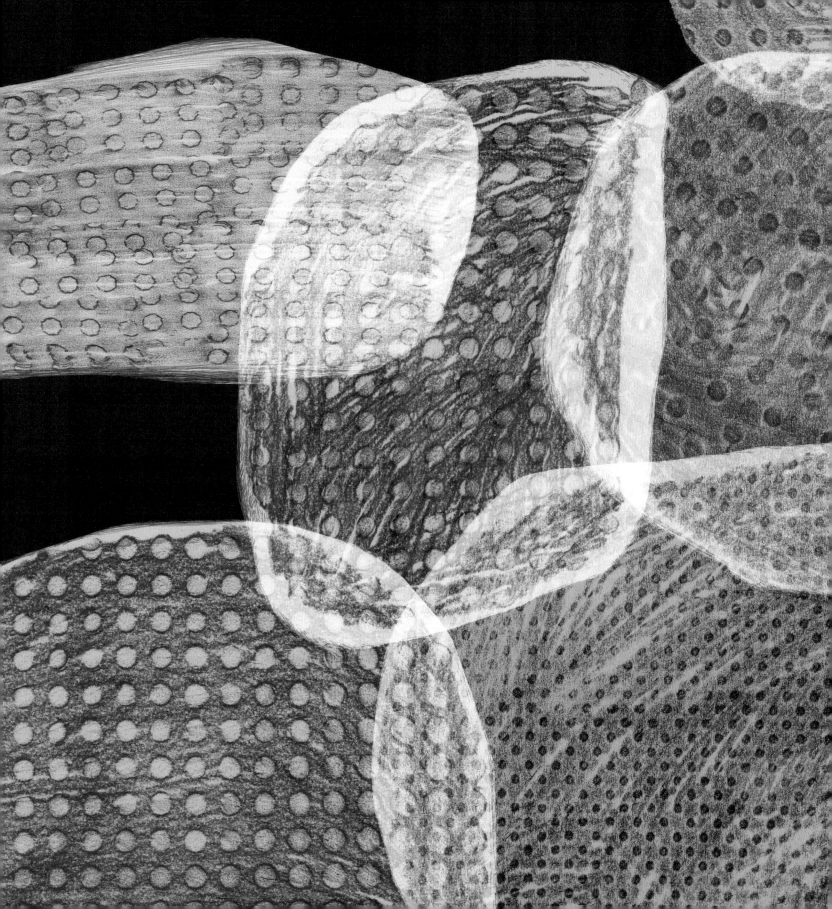

¿Qué estaba diciendo…?

What was I saying…?

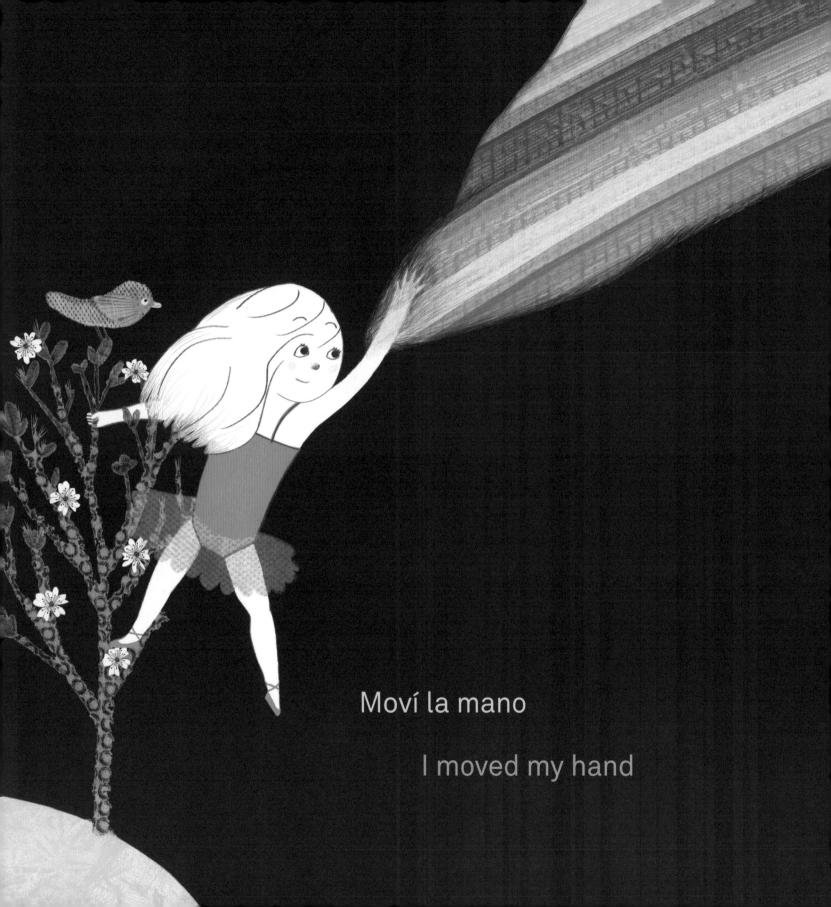

Moví la mano

I moved my hand

¡y encontré el cielo!

and I found the sky!